AIRLOCK

First published 2014 by A & C Black
an imprint of Bloomsbury Publishing Plc
50 Bedford Square
London WC1B 3DP

www.bloomsbury.com

ISBN 978-1-4081-9687-8

A CIP catalogue for this book is available from the British Library.

Printed and Bound by CIP Group (UK) Ltd, Croydon CR0 4YY

1 3 5 7 9 10 8 6 4 2

AIRLOCK

SIMON CHESHIRE

ILLUSTRATED BY
ADRIAN STONE

A & C BLACK
AN IMPRINT OF BLOOMSBURY
LONDON NEW DELHI NEW YORK SYDNEY

Contents

CHAPTER ONE

School Trip

It was the most amazing thing George had ever seen.

He held his breath, hardly daring to move or blink, in case he missed a micro-second of it. Through the wide, oval windows of the passenger cabin, he could see the planet Earth far below him. It looked like a gigantic blue ball, covered in swirling patterns of cloud. Surrounding it was the deep blackness of space, scattered with a sprinkling of bright stars. By craning his neck, George could make out the coastlines of northern Europe.

It felt strange to know that only a couple of hours ago, he'd been standing in the vast CentralCity Air and Space Port looking up at the sky through which he was now travelling. He had gazed at the stars above and wondered what his journey was going to be like. And now, here he was in space!

A delicate chime sounded overhead.

The high, calm voice of the stewardess said, "Ladies and gentlemen, we will shortly be approaching our destination, the *Berners-Lee* Orbital Platform. The shuttle will bank to your left in a moment, and we will have our first sight of the space station. Thank you for travelling MaxiBoost Spaceways. My assistant Roj will soon be handing out free souvenir MaxiBoost baseball caps. Thank you."

George glanced over to where his friends Josh and Amira were sitting. They looked just as excited as him. Amira was intently scrolling through data on her mini-screen, looking up the technical details of the passenger shuttle in which they were travelling, her fold-down table covered in books packed full of MaxiBoost Spaceways trivia. Josh was finishing off the packed lunch he'd brought with him, his jumper covered in crumbs as he licked his lips clean.

"For goodness' sake, Josh," muttered Mr Snodbury. "You were supposed to save that until lunchtime. It said so quite clearly on the letter home to your parents."

"Sorry, Mr Snodbury," said Josh through a mouth full of food, spraying crumbs everywhere as he spoke. "I was hungry."

Mr Snodbury flicked the crumbs off his jacket with a look of distaste on his face. He was George, Josh and Amira's head teacher. There were only two things George wasn't enjoying about this school trip: one was having Mr Snodbury in charge, instead of their form teacher Miss Astro; the other was having Dwayne with them too.

"Mr Snodbury," said Dwayne, as Mr Snodbury brushed the last of the crumbs away, "George ate his packed lunch too. I saw him." Dwayne sneered at George.

"Did you, George?" said Mr Snodbury.

"Umm," said George, going a bit red. "I ate it before we took off from Earth."

Mr Snodbury tutted and shook his head. "I can see I'm going to have to keep a close eye on you. The four of you are representing the school on this trip, and I expect good behaviour and a mature attitude from all of you, at all times. I'm sure Amira hasn't been an oinky pig-wig and gobbled up her packed lunch already, have you, Amira?"

Amira didn't even look away from her mini-screen as she held up the empty packet that had contained her packed lunch. Mr Snodbury sighed. Dwayne showed Mr Snodbury that his packed lunch was completely intact, not so much as nibbled. Then he sneered at George again. George's eyes narrowed. He could see that Dwayne was going to be trouble.

At that moment, the view through the windows suddenly veered to one side. Nobody inside the shuttle felt any movement, because the craft's artificial gravity kept them all safely in their seats. With no air turbulence and no gravity in space, the ride inside the shuttle was as smooth as glass. Only the view outside changed.

George found the sensation of space flight odd but exciting. Mr Snodbury had said it made him want to be sick. As the view through the windows shifted, without giving any other feeling of movement, Mr Snodbury gripped the sides of his seat and went slightly green.

"Are you feeling spacesick again, Mr Snodbury?" asked Amira.

Mr Snodbury simply shut his eyes and nodded.

The shuttle's engines changed tone. Since the spacecraft had left Earth, George had heard a steady, low, pulsing rumble vibrating gently through the ship. Now, as the shuttle turned and manoeuvred, the rumble rose slightly in pitch.

The huge space station *Berners-Lee* glided into view. It was about the size of a block of flats. It was a long, curving structure of steel, wrapped in solar panels. At one end was a bulbous section out of which stuck huge nozzles. At the other end was a box-like section covered in large windows.

It was the most amazing thing George had ever seen. He had studied countless images of it in his school books but to see it in real life was a completely different experience. He held his breath, hardly daring to move or blink.

Mr Snodbury still had his eyes shut.

"Don't miss this, Mr Snodbury," said Amira. "Look, you can see people moving around inside! The station is parked in geostationary orbit at the moment."

Mr Snodbury opened one eye. "Geo... what?"

"Geostationary orbit," explained Amira. "It's when an object is exactly the right distance away from the Earth, so that the pull of the Earth's gravity keeps it in balance."

George demonstrated using empty packed lunch bags to represent the Earth and the space station. "The balance of distance and gravity keeps the station in position above a particular place on the Earth's surface. Clever, isn't it?"

"G-G-Gravity," muttered Mr Snodbury. "B-Balance... Excuse me!"

He dashed for the toilets. George, Josh and Amira shrugged and went back to watching the huge space station get closer and closer.

There were several dozen passengers on today's shuttle flight. Most were scientists and technicians arriving at *Berners-Lee* to work. The return trip, due to leave for Earth in an hour's time, would be full of other scientists and technicians going back home.

George and his friends were going to stay on the station for the rest of the week. This had been their reward for getting the best results in their year's Science class. Amira, as always, had come top of the class and probably knew more about the ship than any member of the crew, while Josh was still amazed that he had passed the exam, never mind coming in the top four.

The shuttle slid into position beside the station. Now George and his friends could no longer see the stars – their whole view was of the solar panels along the station's hull.

A tunnel-like extension emerged from the side of the shuttle and clamped into place around the sliding door which formed the station's main entrance. A hollow KA-KLANG sounded throughout the shuttle.

"Docking Port A sealed," said the calm voice of the stewardess. "You may now move about the cabin, ladies and gentlemen."

Passengers began to stand up and retrieve their luggage from the overhead compartments. Voices began to chatter up and down the cabin. A man in a MaxiBoost Spaceways uniform walked along the aisles between the seats, handing out bright blue baseball caps with the MaxiBoost logo on the front. George, Josh, Amira and Dwayne put theirs on and grinned at each other.

"I feel like a real space technician now," said George.

Dwayne snatched George's cap off his head, ripped the tab at the back so it wouldn't stay on properly, then plonked it back on George's head.

"Now you can feel like a twit," he sniggered.

For a moment, George was too shocked to react. The cap slid down over his eyes.

Mr Snodbury appeared, making his way along the aisle, clutching at the backs of seats as he went. He didn't look quite so green now. He was more a sort of yellowy-white.

"Come on, everyone," he said, unsteadily, "gather up all your stuff."

"Mr Snodbury," protested George, "Dwayne just ripped my baseball cap!"

"Now now, George," muttered Mr Snodbury, steadying himself against the seats and looking like he was doing his best to fight back another wave of sickness.

George glared at Dwayne. Dwayne pulled a ha-ha face at George.

All the passengers shuffled forwards towards the exit, bags and knees bumping. As he approached the airlock joining the shuttle to the space station, George could smell the cool, filtered air pumped out by the station's Atmosphere Purifier.

He felt nervous and excited all over again. Above the exit was a glowing display screen which said: "Thank you for travelling MaxiBoost Spaceways, which is not part of MegaZone Corporation in any way, never has been, never will be, because that lot are rubbish. Have a nice day. Local time is... 11:20am, May 13, 2125."

George couldn't wait to actually set foot on a real space station. It was a dream come true.

Little did he know that, within hours, his dream would become a nightmare.

CHAPTER TwO

The Commander

George's group assembled on the wide walkway that was just beyond the main airlock. Mr Snodbury fussed and fretted, ticking items off from a list on his mini-screen, all the while trying to juggle his luggage which was so badly packed that items kept falling out and rolling away. George looked around, at the gleaming metallic surfaces and flowing displays all around them. His eyes were wide and his jaw seemed to be dangling loosely. He started to wonder if there was any aspect of this space station which *wasn't* going to make him hugely amazed and impressed.

Beside the airlock, the crew of the space shuttle were getting into an argument with a couple of the space station's security guards. They were hissing insults at each other and flapping their baseball caps.

"What's all that about?" whispered Josh.

"Company wars," replied Amira. "MaxiBoost Spaceways and MegaZone Corporation are bitter business rivals. They've bought armies and held battles back home. Haven't you seen it on the newsfeeds?"

"MegaZone built this station, didn't they?" said George.

"Yes," said Amira, "and MaxiBoost were furious that MegaZone got the contract."

Passengers for the return trip to Earth were already filing onto the shuttle. The MaxiBoost shuttle crew went back to their normal, smiling selves as they welcomed the passengers on board.

Two smartly dressed technicians approached George's group: a tall blonde woman and a slightly shorter man with brown curly hair. The woman walked over to Mr Snodbury and held out her hand.

"Hello, I take it you're the group from CentralCity Primary School?" she said, in a voice as smart as her uniform.

"That's right," said Mr Snodbury, shaking her hand. "These are the four Year 6 pupils who've scored the highest marks in Science this year, and so earned a place on this trip. This is Dwayne, George, Amira, and Josh."

The pupils all said hello.

"I'm Jane Parker," said the woman, "and this is Ian Ash. We're on the senior technical staff here at *Berners-Lee* and we've been assigned to look after you while you're here. Follow me."

Parker and Ash moved off down the corridor and George's group trailed them obediently. Space station crew were walking about in all directions, some in overalls, some in uniforms like Parker and Ash. Some of them were pushing heavy equipment on anti-gravity pads, others were checking readouts and adjusting settings. None of them paid the slightest bit of attention to George or his friends. Small groups from schools on Earth visited the space station regularly, so nobody took any notice of these CentralCity Primary visitors.

"We'll start the tour at the crew quarters," said Parker. "You can leave your belongings there."

The crew quarters reminded George of a holiday he'd once spent with his family, staying in a caravan at the seaside. Everything was quite small, and tightly packed in to make maximum use of space. Mr Snodbury and the four pupils each had their own bunk with a small curtain to pull across it for privacy. The washbasin and vacuum-toilet were located at the end of the shared quarters. George placed his belongings neatly in his cabin and glanced over at the others. Mr Snodbury had dumped all of his belongings into a massive heap on his bunk. Everything spilled out of his bag and covered his small bunk. It was going to be difficult living in such small quarters with someone who was so messy for a week.

"There's an instruction booklet on how to use the toilets," said Parker. "Make sure you read it. We had a kid last month who managed to get his bottom wedged in the vacuum pump."

"Why does the loo need a vacuum pump?" whispered Josh with a worried look on his face.

"Recycling," said Amira with a nod and a smile. "Everything has to be recycled up here, it's not like at home where you don't have to worry about it. All waste gets used as biofuel for the fusion reactors which power the station."

"Having a poo keeps the lights on." George grinned.

"That's right," laughed Parker.

Dwayne and Mr Snodbury eyed George carefully. Mr Snodbury didn't like people making jokes of anything, even at the best of times. He certainly didn't approve of mentioning poo on a school trip.

The tour of the space station continued with the storage bays, the engine room, the air filters, the science labs, the fusion reactors, the medical section, the docking ports, the solar stacks, the canteen, the artificial vegetable garden...

Soon, George's head was spinning. He could hardly take it all in. Everyone else's heads must have been spinning too, because several times they had to stop to find a member of the group who'd managed to wander off somewhere. Mr Snodbury had fallen behind the group on countless occasions and had to run each time to catch up while Josh had been found twice in the canteen – he claimed he had gotten lost but George knew better than to believe him, given his overactive appetite.

Jane Parker explained various aspects of life and work on the station as they walked. All four pupils asked lots of questions, especially Amira, who hadn't stopped jotting down notes on her mini-screen since the tour began. Ian Ash said very little during the tour. He seemed much more serious than Parker, and appeared to be in a hurry to go somewhere. George noticed that Ash checked the time more than once.

At last, they came to the highlight of the tour. A tall pair of automatic doors swept aside with a WHOOSH to reveal a large, shiny room in which a dozen scientists monitored various screens and machines. Through banks of windows, George could see the twinkling stars, and the graceful curve of the Earth below. This room was the box-like section George had seen from the shuttle.

"Welcome to the Control Centre," said Parker. "This is the nerve centre of all our activities. It's here that we organise everything we do. We run scientific experiments, we test new ideas in space propulsion and space travel, and we act as a refuelling and stop-off point for spacecraft going to the colonies on the Moon or Mars."

George, Josh and Amira gazed at the flashing lights and beeping machines. Dwayne scratched his armpit. Mr Snodbury ushered them out of the way of passing scientists.

"Don't touch anything," he said. "Goodness knows what might happen if you started fiddling with the controls in here."

Parker walked over to a grumpy-looking man sitting in a large padded chair beside a series of touchscreens. She spoke quietly to him and he looked over at George's group with a scowl. Then he stood up and came over to them.

He was short and square-shaped, with a nose like a turnip. He walked like a bulldog and his uniform displayed a number of small coloured patches signifying various awards and achievements.

"This is Commander Ferguson," announced Parker to the group. "He's in charge of all operations at *Berners-Lee*."

She turned to the Commander. "I've just been giving them the tour, sir. They've been asking some very interesting questions. They're a bright bunch of kids."

Commander Ferguson stared at George's group in silence for a moment. "Bright bunch of kids, yes," he said in a deep voice. "Kids. I don't approve of kids being on my space station. When colonists' ships dock here, I tell them to keep their children on board their vessels. Can't have 'em running about. This is a serious scientific establishment."

"Oh, we're very serious about science," said George. "That's why we're here."

Commander Ferguson leaned forward, until his face was almost level with George's. George could smell aftershave. "We're very serious about science... sir," said the Commander quietly.

"Sorry. We're very serious about science, *sir*." George gulped nervously.

The Commander straightened up again. "I run a tight ship, and I expect everyone on this station to obey the rules and to do things by the book. Is that clear?"

"Yes," said George's group. "Yes, sir!" they quickly corrected themselves. Mr Snodbury dabbed sweat from his forehead with a cotton handkerchief.

The Commander continued: "And obeying the rules and doing things by the book does not include wearing promotional headgear." He pointed at Josh's, Amira's and Dwayne's MaxiBoost baseball caps. George's cap was still sliding around on his head. All four of them whipped their caps off and stuffed them into their pockets.

"This is a MegaZone Corporation facility," said the Commander. "I will not have MaxiBoost logos on my station. Is that clear?"

"Yes, sir," said the four pupils quickly.

The Commander turned to Jane Parker. "What were you thinking, Parker, letting them walk around like that? You should know better."

"Yes, sir, sorry, sir," said Parker, going red.

"If anyone from MegaZone head office had been here, this could have started another trade war. Now get them all out of here. Kids! Huh!"

While the Commander had been telling Parker off, George had noticed something unusual on the Commander's touchscreens. A small progress bar was creeping to the right, and changing colour from green to red.

"Umm, Commander," said George, putting up his hand hesitantly, "you've got a problem in Number 2 fusion reactor."

Commander Ferguson looked over his shoulder at the screen. "Are you trying to tell me my job, boy?"

"No, of course not," said George quietly. "I just thought you ought to know. Doesn't that show an overload alert?"

"It shows a minor imbalance, boy," spluttered the Commander. "Do you think I don't know my own readouts? Get this child out of here, Parker!"

"Yes, sir."

"I think George is right," said Amira. "We've all studied this station in class. That indicator is moving too fast to be a minor imbalance."

"It *is* moving very quickly, sir," said Parker.

The Commander marched over to the screen and began to adjust various settings. "Soon have it sorted out," he barked. "No need to panic."

Parker frowned. "What could possibly cause the reactor to suddenly – ?"

She never finished her sentence. Suddenly, a violent jolt rocked the entire space station. Everyone in the Control Centre was knocked off their feet. From somewhere deep within the station came a rumbling sound.

CHAPTER THREE

Overload

The lights flickered. George felt a rush of fear as the entire station shook again.

"W-what's happened?" cried Mr Snodbury, terrified. "Is that normal?"

"Number 2 reactor has overloaded," said Parker. "Your students were right."

The lights dimmed and flared. Technicians began to run from screen to screen. The doors to the Control Centre slid open and a team of scientists rushed in.

George and his friends were too scared to speak. Finally, George turned to Jane Parker. "Is there anything we can do to help?"

"Stay there, and try to stay calm," said Parker. She dashed across to a machine that was emitting a high-pitched alarm signal. Ian Ash was already there, and together they tried to work out what had gone wrong.

Commander Ferguson barked into a communicator fixed to the sleeve of his uniform. George could hear his voice echo along the space station's corridors.

"This is the Commander. Full emergency procedure. Technical staff to workstations. All departments report in. This is not a drill. I want this done by the book!"

By now, Mr Snodbury was dabbing so much sweat off his face that his handkerchief was wringing wet. George, Josh and Amira looked at each other, frightened by the way that the station's staff were clearly so worried. Even Dwayne was looking nervous.

"Are you OK?" whispered George.

Josh and Amira nodded, with grim expressions on their faces.

The lights returned to their normal brightness. Technicians called out figures and readings to each other. The floor wasn't shaking any more.

Commander Ferguson called over to Ash and Parker. "Report!"

"Overload in reactor 2, Commander," said Ash. "I think we've got it under control."

The Commander turned and was surprised to see George's group huddled in a corner.

"What are those people still doing here? You children, go to your cabins, and stay there until further notice. We've had an emergency situation, but now the emergency is under control. There's nothing to panic about. Our normal routine will continue shortly. There is no cause for concern. None whatsoever. Is that clear? All of you, is that clear?"

George and his friends didn't answer. They were stunned into silence by what they could see through the Control Centre's many large windows. Josh, who had turned ghostly white, pointed at the window with a shaking finger, unable to speak. Commander Ferguson turned to see what he was staring at.

From the left-hand side of the station, drifting slowly into view, came pieces of twisted metal and shards of shattered solar panels. Some were very large, while others were little more than shreds and scraps. They gradually rotated, weightless in space, moving past the Control Centre's windows and off into the distance, shining like metallic dust in the

light from the sun. Behind them, the curve of the Earth glowed blue and bright.

Parker gasped and clapped her hands to her mouth.

"What...?" croaked the Commander, hardly able to believe his eyes.

"That noise we heard must have been an explosion," gasped Josh. "And a big one."

"The overload must have been huge," said Amira. "Think of all those poor people that were out there!" She buried her face in her hands.

Commander Ferguson's voice cut across everyone's thoughts. "Parker! Escort those children to the canteen and keep them there! Ash! Take over in here! I'm going to assess the damage."

"Aye, sir," called Ash. He hurried over to the Commander's touchscreens. Parker ushered George's group out of the room, as the Commander swept past them. He marched out into the corridor.

They hadn't got far before they found their way blocked. An emergency seal, striped red and yellow, had inflated across one of the walkways. A uniformed man was working close by.

"What's happened here?" barked Commander Ferguson.

"The explosion tore a section of the hull open, sir," said the uniformed man. "The reactor controls in corridor B-6 weren't damaged, but walkways B-9, B-10 and B-11 all blew out. These pressure seals will be fine for a while, sir, but they can't last too long. You can get around this blockage by going through the kitchens."

The Commander thought for a moment. "I'm going to inspect the reactor. See why it overloaded. Doesn't make sense."

He marched off in one direction, while Parker, Mr Snodbury and Dwayne went in the direction of the canteen. Josh and Amira were about to head for the canteen too, when George held them back, pressing a finger to his lips to urge them to be quiet.

"Let's follow the Commander," he whispered. "We need to find out what's going on."

"He'll be furious if he sees us," hissed Amira.

"I'm not sure I want to get into any more trouble with the Commander," muttered Josh. "I'm scared enough as it is."

"We're here to discover all we can about the station, aren't we?" said George. "I'm scared too, but I don't want to sit around with nothing to do but read the toilet instructions. I think we ought to do something to help."

"Like what?" whispered Amira.

"Well, er, we don't know that yet, do we?" said George. "We'll just have to see."

With that, he headed off in the direction the Commander had taken. With worried expressions clouding their faces, Josh and Amira took a fleeting look over their shoulders and followed him. They made their way through the station's cramped kitchens, and emerged into a corridor which was cloaked in darkness apart from a line of blue emergency lights set into the floor.

"It's cold in here too," said Josh.

"Maybe the heating system's been damaged as well?" said Amira.

George had reached the far end of the corridor. He turned and put a finger to his lips to silence his friends. Then he pointed around the corner. Josh and Amira crept up behind him.

They all pressed themselves into the shadows, peeking slowly around the corner to see what was going on at the control panels outside the room that housed fusion reactor number 2, the one which had overloaded.

Commander Ferguson was there, talking to Ian Ash. Ash was speaking in a low voice. George and his friends screwed up their faces in concentration, trying to overhear the men's conversation. Once they did, they almost wished they hadn't.

"It's far worse than we thought, sir," said Ash. "Three of this reactor's four fusion chambers exploded. If the fourth had gone too, this area where we're standing would have been vaporised. As it is, the control panels here weren't damaged. They're working normally, although I can't understand how. Sir, I estimate that twenty-five per cent of the entire station has been destroyed."

The Commander stared at Ash in horror. "A quarter of the station, man? Gone?"

"Yes, sir. All the labs and the docking ports. The emergency seals kicked in straight away, but we still lost a huge volume of our atmosphere. There are power outages all over the station. And..."

"And what, Ash?" demanded the Commander.

"Sir, the labs are where most people work. So..."

The Commander was quiet for a second or two. The colour seemed to drain from his face. "How many of the crew did we lose?"

Ash sighed. "Apart from the Control Centre staff," he said at last, "I think there are less than a dozen of us left. All the rest are... floating out there. There isn't even anything we can do to retrieve them."

"Keep a grip, Ash," growled the Commander. "We've got to play this by the book. Follow proper procedures." He ran a trembling hand across his forehead, then straightened up and pulled his uniform straight. "What's the outlook?"

"Bad, sir," said Ash. "Atmosphere, power, all life support systems are damaged."

"Prepare both the escape pods, just in case."

"They went up too, sir, they were next to the docking bays. I've followed the rule book, Commander, so I've called to Earth for a rescue ship. But..."

"But what?" cried the Commander.

"Well, sir, it's MaxiBoost who run the shuttles, and they're insisting that all the correct forms have to be filled in back on Earth before they'll even send for the refuelling truck."

Commander Ferguson slammed his fist into the nearest wall. "Those blasted MaxiBoost fools!" he spat. "They've gone too far this time! Get it sorted! I want that rescue ship on its way!"

He stormed off, Ash following in his wake.

George, Josh and Amira emerged from the shadows. George's heart was thumping.

"This is terrible," wailed Josh. "This trip was supposed to be a reward for coming top of the class. Now it looks like we might never get home again!"

"Try to keep calm," said Amira.

"Not easy," muttered George. "Especially when you realise what caused that explosion."

The other two were puzzled. "They don't know what caused it yet," said Amira.

"I think I do," said George. "Look at these control panels, the ones which operate what's left of the reactor. Ash said they're working fine."

"So?" said Josh.

Amira suddenly remembered something she'd read on her mini-screen, technical information about the station. "Oh no," she whispered.

George nodded his head. "An accidental overload would have fused all these controls. They'd be useless. But here they are, undamaged. The overload could only have been caused by the controls being set that way. That explosion wasn't an accident at all. It was sabotage. Someone did it deliberately."

CHAPTER FOUR

Sabotage

"Who?" cried Josh.

"Why?" cried Amira.

"We'll just have to work that out as we go along," said George. "Right now, we need to tell the Commander what we've discovered."

"He's not going to like this," gulped Josh. "He is really not going to like this."

Josh was right.

A few minutes later, when the three of them arrived back at the Control Centre, they told Commander Ferguson the bad news.

His face flushed with anger. "Sabotage?" he snapped. "On my station? I've never heard such nonsense!"

At that moment Ash arrived, reading figures from a mini-screen.

"Sir," he said, "I've worked out why the explosion happened."

"Oh, I suppose you think it was deliberate too, do you?" scoffed the Commander.

Ash blinked in surprise. "Yes. The reactor's controls would have fused if there had been any accidental... Hang on, did you kids already know that?"

"Proper little smartypants, aren't they?" said the Commander.

"Sorry, sir, I should have worked it out straight away," said Ash. "I guess the whole emergency situation stopped me thinking clearly."

"The situation is that there's a saboteur on board," said George.

"Keep quiet, boy," hissed the Commander, glancing around at the technicians working frantically at their screens. "I don't want talk of sabotage getting out and distracting my staff from their duties."

"So, you believe us now?" said Amira. "Now that Ash has confirmed what we're saying?"

"I believe we've got a remarkable coincidence here," growled Commander Ferguson.

"How do you mean?" said George. He thought he saw what the Commander was getting at, but even thinking about it made his stomach do somersaults.

"I mean," said the Commander, looming over the three students, "that every last member of my crew was selected for duty by me, personally. Every last member of my crew is a highly trained expert in their field, loyal to me and to MegaZone Corporation. I cannot and will not believe that one of them would not only destroy our work here but also cause the deaths of many of their fellow scientists. If there is a saboteur loose on this station, then they're an outsider. And guess what? I have three outsiders standing right in front of me now."

"You can't think one of us did it?" gasped Josh.

"Why not?" said the Commander. "You're all top of the class in Science, aren't you? You've all studied how this station works. The three of you could easily have set that reactor to overload."

"But why?" cried Amira. "What possible reason could we have?"

"Oh, I think there's a very obvious reason," said the Commander in a low voice. "I've already had to question your loyalty once today."

Ash took a step forward. "Those caps," he said. "MaxiBoost baseball caps. Could these kids be spies for MaxiBoost?"

"What?" cried George. "Spies who wear the logo of who they're spying for? Don't be daft!"

"It could be some sort of bluff," said the Commander. "A feeble attempt to divert suspicion. Here's that remarkable coincidence I mentioned: Fact one, outsiders arrive; fact two, only outsiders would sabotage this station; fact three, within a couple of hours of outsiders arriving, this station has been sabotaged. Do you follow my logic?"

"Y-yes," stammered George, a feeling of terror sending icy shivers up his spine. "But we didn't do it! Why would we sabotage the station and then tell you about it?"

Ash ignored him and turned to the Commander. "It would make sense for them to be spies, sir," he said. "MaxiBoost tried all kinds of underhand tricks during the company wars. They certainly wouldn't hesitate to use kids as spies. They could send them on board, undercover, posing as school trippers. Then they could secretly sabotage the station and we'd be forced to call in a rescue shuttle. A MaxiBoost rescue shuttle. The station would be disabled, and MegaZone Corporation would get blamed for running things badly, maybe even lose the contract to build in space. Meanwhile, the undetected saboteurs could simply sneak away on the rescue shuttle along with the remains of the station crew."

"That's not how it is!" cried Amira. "We're not spies for anyone!"

The Commander loomed over them. "Are you trying to ruin me? Were you sent here to wreck my career? Were you?"

"No, we swear!" said Josh.

"Well, there's a sure way to find out," said Ash. "I can run a DNA spectrum test on the reactor's control panels. That'll tell us exactly who's been near those controls in the last twenty-four hours."

"Get to it, Ash," barked the Commander.

"How can they tell that?" hissed Josh to George and Amira.

Amira leaned towards him to whisper her answer. "DNA is your genes, the biological recipe that's in every cell of your body. If someone handles something, or even stands beside it, microscopic bits of skin, and hair, and stuff from your hands, all kinds

41

of things, end up on and around where you've been. Using the right equipment, you can detect even tiny little particles of it. That's why there's so little crime back on Earth these days. The cops can work out exactly who was where, when, and what they did."

"Stop that whispering!" cried Commander Ferguson. "More scheming? I've heard quite enough from you three. Stand there, where I can see you, and don't move. You can consider yourselves under arrest, until the rescue ship arrives."

At that moment, Mr Snodbury came bustling in. "Ah! There you are! You three were supposed to stay with me and Jane Parker. I'm so sorry, Commander, I hope they've not been making a nuisance of themselves."

Commander Ferguson slowly turned to face Mr Snodbury. The expression on his face declared that he'd had about all he could stand for one day. Within a matter of minutes, he and Mr Snodbury were having a heated discussion on the topic of George, Josh and Amira.

While Mr Snodbury was squawking things such as "Under arrest?" and "Outrageous accusation!" George turned his attention to other matters.

"Where's Dwayne got to, I wonder?" he muttered to himself. Making sure that the Commander wasn't looking in his direction, George nudged Amira with his elbow. "Does this station have security cameras?"

"Yes, I think so," said Amira. "I don't know how many will still be working."

"Can you hack into the camera system with your mini-screen?"

"Sure, easy." She booted up some software, entered some data, and up popped a picture of the corridor outside the Control Centre. "Here. You can flick between cameras by pressing this button."

"Thanks," said George, taking the mini-screen and tapping his way through various views. At last, he found what he was looking for. A thin, furtive figure was sneaking along towards the crew quarters. The image from the camera was jumpy and crackling, but George could clearly see that the figure was Dwayne.

"I knew it," he muttered. "I knew you'd be trouble. Why are you sneaking back to the cabins?"

Could Dwayne have been responsible for the explosion? Was he secretly working for MaxiBoost Spaceways?

George passed the mini-screen to Josh and Amira and pointed at the figure of Dwayne. A look of shock and surprise flashed across their faces.

"You don't think – " Amira began.

ZZAAA – ZZAAA – ZZAAA –

Before they had time to discuss the theory any further, an emergency siren filled the air. George almost jumped out of his skin. Technicians dashed

across the Control Centre, gathering around a screen which was flashing warnings and a series of numbers rapidly counting down from 65%.

"One of the emergency seals has given way!" cried one of the crew to the Commander. "We're losing oxygen fast!"

"Cut in the back-ups!" called the Commander.

"I can't, sir, they run on power from reactor 2. There's no way to engage the air pump."

Mr Snodbury cowered in terror behind one of the workstations.

"Where's the manual over-ride?" cried the Commander. "If we don't get the back-ups working we'll all suffocate!"

"It's on the other side of corridor B-11, sir... so, since the explosion, it's now out in space."

George clapped his hands to his ears to block out the din of the alarm. The station was becoming more than simply a space-wreck in need of rescue. Its systems were starting to break down. It was rapidly turning into a death trap.

CHAPTER FIVE

Lost in Space

Ash returned to the Control Centre accompanied by Parker, just as the alarm was silenced by a sharp order from the Commander.

Ash brandished a small metallic device in his hand.

"I've scanned the reactor's panels, Commander," he said. "The scanner is just analysing the results. Then we'll know who caused the explosion."

"No time for that now, Ash!" blustered the Commander. "We have to get the back-up air pumps working. You and I will have to spacewalk around the outside of the station. Parker, you're in charge of switching the air supply inside. And take charge of those blasted kids!"

"Stick with me, you three," said Jane Parker to George and his friends. "I'll need you to operate the pumps, nobody can be spared from in here."

As they left the Control Centre, George looked back at the scattering of staff hunched over their screens. He was feeling worried and frightened, but they looked even more worried and frightened. Several of them were calling out various readings to each other.

Mr Snodbury was cowering behind a bank of computers, frantically trying to connect a phone call with his mini-screen and getting nothing but a 'No Signal' response.

Less than two minutes later, Ian Ash and Commander Ferguson were climbing into spacesuits as fast as they could. Parker was beside them, ready to operate the airlock through which Ash and the Commander could reach the outside of the station. Behind her, George, Josh and Amira stood ready at the controls of the back-up air pumps.

"Why have they got to get outside?" asked Josh. "Can't they fix the air supply from in here?"

"No," said Amira. "The explosion destroyed half the mechanism. They've got to find a big air pipe

47

that's dangling out there, and connect it up to the station by hand. Then we can switch the air supply over from these controls."

"And if they don't manage it," said George, "we'll start running short of air to breathe in a matter of minutes."

Parker pulled a lever and the airlock door slid aside with a hiss. Ash and the Commander clicked the helmets of their suits into place. They both tapped the sides of their helmets and shook their heads.

"Communicators aren't working," said Parker. "Minor problem, I guess, compared to everything else."

The two bulky figures shuffled into the airlock. Coloured lights blinked on the large, rectangular packs attached to their backs. Small jet nozzles poked out of the packs – these were what they would use to move around in space.

The airlock door hissed shut, Parker operated a second lever, and the outer door in front of Ash and the Commander glided silently back. Through a clear panel in the airlock door, George could see them switch on their backpacks and jet out into the inky blackness beyond.

"Keep an eye on that indicator," said Parker, pointing to a tall red panel just above George's head. "When it goes green, the pipe's been connected. Then we switch the pumps on."

Using her mini-screen, Amira tried to tap into the sensors outside the station, so that they could see what Ash and the Commander were doing.

All she could get was a fuzz of static. "They must be broken," she said. "Like the suit communicators."

They waited. Without being able to see or hear the men outside, they felt more tension with every passing second. Half the lights had fused along the corridor in which they stood. The shiny walls and floor had seemed sleek and high-tech only a few hours earlier. Now they seemed gloomy and sinister. The corridor was eerily quiet.

George started wondering where Dwayne had got to. Why had he been sneaking back to the crew cabins? What was he up to right now?

Suddenly, Josh cried out. "Oh no! Look!"

They gathered at the window in the airlock door. To their horror, they could see a spacesuit spinning rapidly away from the station, shooting further and further into the distance. It was Ash.

A loud PING sounded behind George. The red panel had turned green. The Commander must have managed to connect up the air supply.

"George, switch on the pumps!" called Parker.

George entered a code into the panel in front of him. There was a sharp thump, and from the machinery in the walls came an unsteady throbbing sound.

At that moment, Commander Ferguson collided with the airlock window. He thumped against it with a heavily gloved hand. Parker closed the outer door and then opened the inner one to let the Commander in. He tumbled forward, clutching at his space helmet. Josh and Amira helped him to remove it.

"Ash's backpack blew," he gasped. "I saw a flash."

"But the packs on those suits are MegaZone Premium-A," said Parker. "They're normally very reliable."

"Well, that one wasn't!" snapped the Commander. "Another of my crew gone!"

Parker was clearly upset. The Commander, on the other hand, seemed to be lost in thought.

George was struck by another of those icy feelings of fear. He quickly turned to Josh and Amira and ushered them into a corner of the room.

"I just thought of something, guys. I know we were wondering about whether Dwayne was the saboteur, but what if we're wrong? What if the saboteur was Commander Ferguson himself?"

"What?" said the others together.

"Think about it – Ash had just gathered vital DNA evidence, which would help reveal the identity of the person who'd caused the explosion. What if that person was the Commander? What if he fought with Ash, outside the station, when they were both out of sight and cut off from all communication? What if he'd done something to Ash's backpack? What if the Commander got rid of Ash in order to get rid of the evidence too?" George blurted out in a hushed voice.

Josh and Amira looked stunned. The idea seemed absurd.

"Why would the Commander want to wreck his own space station?" whispered Amira. She paused. "But then again, as Parker said, those backpacks are very reliable. I've read all about the countless tests they go through before they are fit for human use. Isn't it a strange coincidence that precisely the evidence needed to find the saboteur was in the pocket of the person whose backpack went wrong?"

"Or maybe Ash was the saboteur?" suggested Josh. "Suppose the Commander realised this and arranged an 'accident', in order to hide the fact that one of his loyal crew members was a spy?"

George and Amira nodded eagerly.

"What if Ash's backpack break-down was all a con?" continued Amira. "Could he have secretly set his backpack to shoot him far out into space? What if, at this very moment, he's linking up with a shuttle somewhere, instead of tumbling to his death?"

They all looked at each other.

Josh said, "Now I don't have a clue what's going on."

Just then, Dwayne appeared around the corner. "Where have you been?" said Amira.

"None of your business." Dwayne went slightly red.

"Parker," said Commander Ferguson. "I thought I told you to watch these kids?"

"They were helping me operate the air pumps, sir," said Parker. "We're safe. George switched the back-up feed on for me."

The Commander sniffed and cocked his head to one side. The machinery behind the panel George had operated was still making that strange, unsteady noise.

"Did he now?" said Commander Ferguson. "Parker, why are those pumps sounding like an ancient steam engine?"

"It's possible they could have been – " began Parker.

With an almighty cracking sound, the wall beside them suddenly buckled and bulged inwards. The lights in the corridor spluttered and died.

"What's happening now?" cried Josh. "Surely things can't get any worse?"

CHAPTER SIX

Falling to Earth

Things were getting much worse.

There was an electrical fault in the air supply line that the Commander and Ash had fixed. Outside the space station, the supply line had burst into a shower of gas and sparks. The fault was an overload, caused by the various power level problems the station had experienced since the explosion.

Thick jets of air were blasted out into space. The entire station rocked and shuddered.

Within seconds, a rapid series of electrical discharges spread across the outer hull of the station. In the escaped oxygen, bright blue arcs of energy flickered silently against the blackness and the stars.

The lights behind the station's many portholes and windows began to go out. The effect rippled out from the point at which the air supply had short-circuited. Soon it reached the front of the station.

If anyone had been watching the Control Centre from space, they would have seen every screen and machine suddenly rupture and burst into flames. The entire Control Centre became a sizzling, white-hot inferno in seconds.

The station was battered by another shuddering movement from inside. The Control Centre's windows all shattered at the same moment, and the huge room was half-torn from the body of the station. It hung at an angle, like the broken head of a child's doll.

Slowly, so slowly at first that the change was hardly visible, the crippled hulk of the *Berners-Lee* space station began to shift its orbit. The sudden burst of air that had jetted from its side was knocking it off-course. The jet had given it a sharp push, like a swimmer pushing back against the side of a pool.

In the wide corridor where Commander Ferguson, Jane Parker and the Year 6s were getting unsteadily to their feet, it didn't take long to work out what had happened. Even Dwayne and the Commander were looking scared out of their wits.

Mr Snodbury and two technicians appeared, staggering along in the faint glow of the emergency lights set into the floor. All three were streaked with grime. One of the technicians clutched his arm, which was badly scorched.

"W-we were just leaving the Control Centre," gasped Mr Snodbury, his eyes staring. "We got out a second before the whole place went up!"

"The Control Centre doors have sealed, sir," said one of the technicians to Commander Ferguson. "Everything's gone."

George suddenly realised he was breathing much too fast. He screwed up his face for a moment, and tried to steady his nerves. His heart felt like a hammer beating inside his chest. Gritting his teeth, he fought back the emotion that threatened to leak from his eyes and crumple his mouth.

"This is it?" roared the Commander. "Nine of us left? Four crew, four kids and that wet drip of a teacher? We're finished!"

George suddenly felt a rush of anger and determination. "We are not going to give up!" he cried.

"He's right, Commander," said Parker. "The rescue shuttle is on its way. There's still a chance."

"Amira," said George. "Log onto any of the station's sensors that are still working. Find out how far off-course we are."

Amira's fingers tapped at her mini-screen. "We're falling towards Earth at an increasing speed," she said. "The planet's gravity is pulling us in."

"*Berners-Lee* was built in space," said Parker. "It was never designed to land, or even travel out of Earth's orbit."

"As we enter the atmosphere," said Amira, "the station will burn up, and break up."

George tried to keep his voice steady. He didn't make a very good job of it. "How long before that happens?"

"It's hard to say," said Amira. "But from what I can tell, less than an hour."

"That is, if we don't suffocate first," cried the Commander. "The air's already getting thin in here. We must have lost most of it to space. I told you. We're finished."

Mr Snodbury let out a loud yelp of fright. He held his handkerchief across his face.

"Couldn't we push ourselves back into orbit?" said Josh. "Maybe a jet of air from the opposite side of the station would do it?"

"We'd need to use every last bit of air we've got," said Amira. "Which means, even if it worked, we'd die."

"Couldn't we produce a push some other way?" said Josh. "I mean, this station has engines. It can move around."

Parker checked one of the flickering readouts on the wall. "The main engine block is still in one piece, but there's nowhere near enough power left in it to get us free of the Earth's pull. It's down to a few per cent. We mustn't lose heart. The shuttle will already be on its way."

"Then get it here!" cried the Commander, beads of sweat running down his forehead. "Get it here, for goodness' sake!"

The two technicians helped Parker to rig up a communications circuit using Amira's mini-screen wired into what was left of the station's electronics. Eerie creaks and groans echoed from other parts of the station.

"It's getting cold in here," muttered Josh.

"Yes," said George. "I should think most of the systems are dead. There's very little power left. We must try to breathe slowly and steadily, to conserve the remaining air."

Amira's mini-screen flickered and hissed. Parker boosted its signal as far as it would go. "This is *Berners-Lee* station, calling rescue shuttle. Do you read me? This is *Berners-Lee*."

A voice crackled from the mini-screen. "We read you, *Berners-Lee*. This is the MaxiBoost shuttle *Adventurer*. You're very faint. What's your situation?"

"Very bad and getting worse, *Adventurer*. We need immediate help! Are you on your way? I repeat, we need immediate help!"

"Confirm, *Berners-Lee*, we are *en route*," crackled the voice. "Don't worry. We're at full speed. Everything's at maximum. We'll be with you in just ninety minutes."

George felt as if his stomach had turned to water. A terrible, empty feeling suddenly swallowed him up.

Less than an hour, Amira had said. The shuttle wouldn't arrive in time. It would be too late. They'd all be dead.

CHAPTER SEVEN

Saboteur

Out of the corner of his eye, George spotted Dwayne slinking away along the corridor. Dwayne was heading back to the crew cabins again. This time, George was determined to find out what he was up to.

"George, where are you going?" whispered Josh.

"I'm not going to let Dwayne out of my sight for a second," said George. "All this could have been his fault. You stay here, try to help the others come up with a survival plan."

Keeping his distance, George crept along, staying close to the wall. It wasn't difficult for him to remain out of sight, because so few lights were working now. George's footsteps were hidden by the sounds of distant alarms and automated warning voices.

Ahead of him, Dwayne could only be spotted when he passed through patches of light shining dimly from one surface or another. Now and again he threw a glance over his shoulder. George froze, concealed in shadow, until Dwayne moved on.

Soon, they arrived at the crew quarters. Most were still in one piece, although the temperature here was even lower than elsewhere, and the lights were flickering, making the room feel much darker than before.

Dwayne sneaked into his cabin.

George crept up as close as he dared and listened. There was a rustling sound, and the noise of a locker being opened. Was Dwayne about to signal to someone? Was he retrieving some sort of spy equipment? Maybe something that would help him escape the station? Maybe even a weapon, with which to control the station's survivors?

George thought that the best idea would be to catch Dwayne by surprise. That way, Dwayne would be off his guard and George might be able to snatch away whatever Dwayne was holding.

He silently counted to three, then leapt into the cabin.

"Hold it!" he yelled.

Dwayne squealed in fright. He scrambled up onto his bunk, his legs bicycling in mid-air, clutching the item from his locker to his chest.

At once, George realised that Dwayne definitely wasn't the saboteur. Clutched to Dwayne's chest was not a communicator or a weapon, but a small and slightly grubby rectangle of material.

"You frightened the life out of me," cried Dwayne. Then he noticed that George had spotted the piece of material. He went as red as a slice of pickled beetroot.

"Is that why you've kept coming back here?" said George.

"Yes," said Dwayne, in a tiny voice. "It's... my snuggly. I've had it since I was a baby." His head dipped and tears began to slide down his cheeks. "I'm so scared. You'll all laugh at me now because I need my snuggly."

George sat down beside him. "No we won't," he said. "You're not the only one who's frightened, you know. We all are."

Dwayne glanced at him. "Why are you being nice? I ripped your baseball cap. I'm always mean and sneaky with everyone."

George shrugged his shoulders and thought for a moment. "Yes, I suppose you are always mean and sneaky. But that doesn't mean it has to stay that way. Nobody's going to laugh at you."

He stood up. "Come on, we've got to get back to the others."

Dwayne stuffed his snuggly into his pocket, and wiped his eyes on his sleeve. They started to make their way out of the cabin. At that moment, the station began to shake. Things fell off bunks and shelves all around the crew quarters.

"I think we've just reached the outer layer of Earth's atmosphere," said George. "It's going to start getting very bumpy now. We'd better hurry."

They were about to leave when George felt something hit the side of his foot. A badly packed travel bag had tumbled across the floor beside him, and a mini-screen had tumbled out of the bag and landed next to where he was standing. He picked it up, read what was on it, and realised he'd found something very important indeed.

The two of them hurried back to the others as fast as they could. The station was beginning to shudder alarmingly.

"They'll have come up with a plan by now," said George. "Just you wait and see. They're all clever people and they'll be working together, as a team, to get us out of this."

They arrived at the corridor to find everyone in the middle of a fierce argument. Everyone had a different idea about what they should do, or not do, or could do.

Commander Ferguson was pacing back and forth like a caged lion. "So much for the rule book! So much for regulations! We've followed procedure. And it's got us nowhere!"

Panic was setting in. George decided that they needed something to snap them out of it, something to focus their attention.

"You may be interested to know..." he shouted.

Everyone stopped talking and looked at him. The station trembled and shook under their feet. When he saw he'd got their attention, George continued: "You may be interested to know that we can now identify the saboteur. We know who caused all this." He held up the mini-screen he'd found. "I have proof."

"Who was it then?" barked the Commander.

George turned to a figure who was huddled in a corner. "I'm afraid it was you, Mr Snodbury."

CHAPTER EIGHT

One Way Out

"W-what?" cried Mr Snodbury. "What proof could you possibly have?"

George held up the mini-screen. "This is yours, Mr Snodbury. It fell out of your travel bag. It's got instructions on it for causing an overload in a fusion reactor."

"How dare you!" declared Mr Snodbury loudly. "I've never been so..." His words tailed off and he slumped like a deflating balloon. He hung his head in his hands. "You're right," he wailed. "It was me. What have I done? I never thought it would be this bad. They told me the station would only be without power for a few days. They never said there'd be an explosion."

"Who said?" growled Commander Ferguson. "Who are you working for?"

"MaxiBoost Spaceways," said Mr Snodbury. "They offered me a huge amount of money. And I took it. They said they wanted this station to go wrong, so MegaZone Corporation would look bad and MaxiBoost would get the contract to build space stations instead. They told me it would only cause a power failure, I swear! I never wanted all this to happen. They said nobody would get hurt."

"What about Ash?" interrupted Amira. "I've read about those backpacks countless times. They're foolproof."

"That had nothing to do with me, honestly! That must have been a one in a million faulty pack. They said everyone would be fine. But now they've left me here to die, the miserable so-and-so's."

"To get you out of the way," said Parker, "and hide the fact that you were working for them."

With a yell of rage, Commander Ferguson grasped Mr Snodbury by the collar and hauled him to his feet.

"You worm!" he roared. "Give me one good reason I shouldn't tear you limb from limb!"

"Because that won't help!" cried George. "Time is running out. We have to work together. We have to think!"

The Commander pushed Mr Snodbury aside with an angry grunt. "What's there to think about? Life support is all but gone, every system in this station is wrecked and the rescue shuttle will miss us by half an hour!"

A couple of sudden tremors added to the shuddering motion all around them.

George stepped right up to the Commander. "You might be giving up," he said, "but I'm not." He turned to Amira. "Can you work out how long we've got now?"

After a few calculations, Amira said, "The station will break apart in about twenty minutes."

"OK," said George. "Let's think. Is there anything we can use to get clear of the station?"

"Nothing," said Parker. "The two escape pods were destroyed in the first explosion, remember. And the only spacesuit we've got is the one the Commander used."

"Will whopping great chunks of this place hit the Earth?" said Josh.

"No," said Parker. "When the station breaks up, most of it will burn away as it falls. I expect it'll look like a shower of meteorites from the ground."

"Most of it?" said George. "Will some parts of the station stay intact?"

"Maybe a few sheets of metal," said Parker.

Josh suddenly perked up. "What about the main engine housing? Those things are made of micro-bonded carbon fibre. I read it in the technical manual on the way up this morning."

George and Amira stared open-mouthed at Josh, amazed that he had remembered such useful information.

Parker thought for a moment. "I suppose the container holding the main engine is the toughest part of the station. Yes, I expect it would probably reach Earth in one piece. But if it fell in one of the oceans, it would sink to the bottom, and if it hit land it would smash apart instantly. By the time it reached ground level, it would be falling at several hundred kilometres an hour."

"But perhaps we could hide inside it?" said Josh. "At least we'd survive the fall."

"And then either drown or get squished," said Amira. "No thanks."

The rattling and rocking of the station was becoming ever more violent. The corridor was feeling even colder. Everyone's breath was beginning to steam. Very soon, the reverse would happen, and the temperature would rise sharply. The outer hull of the station would heat up to melting point as it tore through Earth's atmosphere.

Mr Snodbury curled up into a ball. "I'm sorry," he mumbled. "I'm so sorry."

"Why did you do it?" said George. "Just for the money?"

"I wanted to leave teaching," sniffed Mr Snodbury. "I've always wanted to run my own gardening centre. But I never had the cash. And now look what I've done. I've destroyed this magnificent space station and killed innocent people. Even with all our technology, space is still a dangerous place. Remember that project we did on the twentieth-century Apollo missions? They had little more than a giant tin can and a pocket calculator, but they got to the Moon and back. From Apollo 11 to *Berners-Lee*, a story of great achievement. And I've just ruined it. I'm glad I can't go back to Earth – I don't deserve to go back! I couldn't face telling everyone what I've done."

Suddenly, George let out a cry. "That's it!" He leapt up. "I know what we can do! I know how we can use that engine housing to survive! And you will come back, Mr Snodbury, we all will."

"Well, we'd better do it quick," said Amira, pointing to her mini-screen. "I've done a few more calculations. It isn't only our lives at stake now. When the station breaks up, it will be directly over northern Europe. When that engine hits the ground, it's going to smash right into the centre of CentralCity. It could even hit the district where we live!"

CHAPTER NINE

Only Chance

The remains of the space station fell towards Earth, faster and faster. The nine survivors inside were shaken and buffeted until they thought their teeth would fall out. A howling whine was steadily rising all around them, as the air outside screeched against the station's hull.

"Parker!" called George above the din. "Can you and the two technicians undo every bolt that holds the main engine compartment in place?"

"Yes, but – ?"

"Just do it, I'll explain later! Everyone else, listen! Collect up anything you can that's soft. Cushions, blankets, anything at all. Get moving, we've only got a few minutes!"

The crew cabins were quickly stripped of pillows and bedclothes. Parker and the technicians hurried to the engine room and loosened everything that held the main engine in place.

The engine housing was about the size of a small school bus, cylindrical in shape and covered in a network of pipes, dials and screens. Two-thirds of the cylinder, from which jutted a series of stubby tubes, was the engine itself. The other third was a chamber in which there was a complex system for keeping the engine running at the correct speed and temperature. There was a hatch at the end of the cylinder, through which technicians would regularly crawl to carry out checks and maintenance.

"We need to pad out the maintenance chamber as much as we can," said George. "We'll get bashed around against all the equipment in there if there isn't anything to cushion us."

"What's the point of being cushioned against all the bashing about we'll get on the way down," said Josh, throwing some pillows in through the hatch, "if we're just going to hit the ground with a huge splat?"

The engine's maintenance chamber was a tight squeeze for five adults and four kids. George found himself squashed tightly beside a small porthole, wedged between Mr Snodbury and Amira. The hatch was pulled shut with a clang and sealed by turning a metal wheel at its centre.

Inside, the noise of the rapidly crumbling station was dulled, but the shuddering tremor of the falling station felt even worse in this confined space.

"Now we wait for the station to break up," said Parker. "Any minute now. George, you'd better tell everyone what you've told me. Your idea for saving our lives."

"This engine housing is much heavier at one end," said George. "The end with the actual engine in it. So we know it will fall engine-first, right?"

"Right," said Amira.

"Remember what Parker told us a while ago? That there's still some power left in the engine. Not very much, but some."

"There's nowhere near enough power to let us fly this thing to the ground, if that's what you're thinking," said the Commander.

"I know," said George, "but when Mr Snodbury mentioned the old Apollo space missions, way back in the twentieth century, it reminded me how they managed to survive a fall through the atmosphere. On the Apollo 11 flight to the Moon, the three astronauts only had a tiny pod in which to return to Earth. It fell through the atmosphere, very fast, heating up like mad. Just like this engine housing is going to do. Then, when they were a few thousand metres above the ground, three parachutes opened which slowed their fall. They splashed down safely in the sea."

"We don't have parachutes," said Josh.

"But we have enough power for one good burst from the engine," said George. "Instead of having parachutes reduce our speed, we wait until we're approaching the ground, then blast every last bit of power we've got left out of the engine. The downward push should slow us enough. We'll still hit the ground with a big bump, but in theory, we'll survive. Well, we should survive. Well, we might survive."

"You've got to admit, sir," said Parker to the Commander, "it's a genius idea. I'd never have thought of it."

"It's crackpot," muttered the Commander. "A dozen things could go wrong. We could start spinning out of control. We could fire the engine too late. Or too early. We could – "

"But it's a chance," said Parker. "It alters our chances from zero to, well, OK, only about twenty per cent, but it's better than nothing."

"This is a twin-pulsed ion thruster," said the Commander. He twisted his head to look at a screen close to his jaw. "At... two point four per cent power, you'll have less than seven seconds of kick."

Suddenly, the engine rocked wildly. The sounds of twisting metal made George's stomach lurch. Light shone through the porthole beside him. He could see large sections of the station drifting away. Each broken section was wrapped in searing white flame, trailing smoke and debris.

Behind them, George could see the graceful curve of the Earth, the horizon gradually flattening as they fell closer and closer to the surface. He felt terrified.

He turned to look at the others. A couple of them had their eyes screwed up tightly. Dwayne pulled his snuggly from his pocket, looked at it for a moment, then tucked it behind him to add to the padding of pillows and blankets. He looked up at George and gave him a feeble smile. George gave him a thumbs-up.

Parker was tapping at Amira's mini-screen. "About three minutes to impact," she said. "We'll have to boot the engine manually. George, you see that little black and yellow plastic cover, just above you?"

"Yes?"

"Flick it up, but don't press the switch beneath. That fires the power cells."

George did as he was told. The switch was small. It seemed so unimportant. But all their lives rested

on it. And possibly the lives of many people down in CentralCity too.

"Two minutes forty seconds," said Parker. "We fire at five kilometres from ground level. You got that?"

"Yes," nodded George.

"I'll count you down."

The engine housing dropped through the sky like a stone. By now, it too was shedding flames. The occupants were rattled from side to side. All around them was the howling roar of the air, like a screaming dragon diving to its death.

"One minute fifty."

Through the porthole, George could see coastlines and ocean, just as he had from the shuttle that morning. They grew closer every second. He felt as if his heart would leap from his throat.

"One minute ten. Get ready!"

Mr Snodbury had the back of his head pressed against a cushion, and his fists clenched so tight that his knuckles were white. Josh and Amira kept their gaze fixed on the porthole, their faces grim and blanched. The Commander held his hand across his chest.

"Ten kilometres above target height..." yelled Parker above the roar. "Nine... eight... stand by to fire, George... seven... six..."

George looked up at the switch.

"Five... four..."

He raised his hand. It juddered as the engine rocked.

"Three..."

The ground was shooting up towards them.

"Two... one..."

George's finger hovered unsteadily above his head.

"Fire!"

He flicked the switch. Instantly, the engine housing bucked as the machinery underneath burst into life. The sudden braking effect pressed them all painfully into whatever was below them. The engine flared with a throbbing WHOOSH. Bright greeny-blue light washed around the porthole.

George thought he would be crushed to death. His whole body felt as if it weighed tonnes. The pulsing of the engine filled the air with static, and there was a sharp smell of electricity.

Then it cut out. Suddenly there was silence.

"Power gone," gasped Parker. "Thirty metres off the ground! Brace yourselves!"

George felt a yawning sensation, like a sudden dip on a rollercoaster.

Then the engine housing, battered, scorched and steaming, hit the ground with a crunching, shattering sound. The jolt made everyone yelp with pain. The engine tottered and rolled, crashing onto its side and scraping along the ground for twenty metres or more. Through the porthole, George could see what looked like the surface of a road.

Everyone groaned and stretched their limbs carefully. The impact had dislocated Parker's shoulder, but apart from that they seemed to have suffered only cuts and bruises.

The Commander reached over and turned the wheel on the hatch. It fell back with a hiss. Cool, clean air flowed into the compartment from outside.

One by one, they crawled out. The engine housing was a crumpled, fire-ravaged piece of junk. Where it had hit the ground was a small crater, and a deep furrow marked where it had skidded.

George, Josh and Amira looked around themselves, feeling dizzy and slightly sick. They were standing in the middle of an ordinary street. On both sides, people were staring out of windows at them, goggle-eyed. From the distance came the sound of approaching sirens.

CHAPTER TEN

Commander

Minutes later, the battered engine housing was surrounded by police, ambulance crews and amazed sightseers. The nine survivors of the *Berners-Lee* were sitting on raised stretchers, wrapped in blankets and being attended to by medics.

A van drew up and a TV news team piled out. They barged their way through the crowd of onlookers and approached Commander Ferguson, camera and microphone pointed in his direction.

"Get out of my face!" he growled.

The news team did a smart U-turn and looked for someone else to interview. Mr Snodbury spotted them, and moved aside the nurse who was seeing to the scratches on his forehead.

"Over here!" he called.

The news team descended upon him like a flock of vultures.

"Can you tell us your name?" gushed the reporter, holding a microphone under Mr Snodbury's nose. "How do you feel? What happened on the *Berners-Lee*? How did you feel?"

Mr Snodbury looked over at George and his friends for a moment, then took a deep breath. "My name is Snodbury. What happened was that I deliberately sabotaged the space station. I caused the deaths of most of its crew, and the destruction of the station itself. I did it because MaxiBoost Spaceways paid me to do it. They lied to me about the effect my actions would have. They intended that MegaZone Corporation would lose business as a result."

For a second or two, the news team were too stunned to speak. They weren't used to someone accepting blame or being honest. Then a dozen people all started to talk at once, and Mr Snodbury was lost in a jostle of legs and voices.

George saw Commander Ferguson approaching him, and felt a fresh wave of nerves. The Commander sat down beside him.

"I want a word with you, George," he said.

"Oh yes?" gulped George.

The Commander glanced around, taking in the scene. "There's going to be a lot of fallout from today. MaxiBoost will be in big trouble. I'll be asked a lot of questions. Before all that happens, there's something I want to say to you."

"Oh yes?" gulped George.

The Commander reached up to his shoulder, to where his Commander's badge of rank was sewn to his uniform. Taking a firm grip on it, he tore it off.

"You saved nine lives today, boy," he said. "You're a hero. You kept your head, you took charge, and you got us home by throwing away the rule book. This belongs to you."

He handed George the badge. It showed a logo of a ship zooming through the stars, and beneath it, in proudly silvery letters, were the words "V.C. Ferguson – COMMANDER – Berners-Lee Orbital Platform."

"I'm sure you worked very hard to get this," said George.

"So did you," said Commander Ferguson.

"Thanks." George smiled.

The Commander patted him on the back and walked away. George waited until the Commander was out of sight before he let his face show how much that pat had hurt his aching, battered muscles.

Amira was sitting on the stretcher next to George. "Just because you're a hero and a senior officer of the space service," she said, "it doesn't mean you can start bossing us about."

Josh was sitting the other side of George. "He's going to be a right big-head now, isn't he," he sighed.

"He can be as much of a big-head as he likes," said Dwayne, who was passing them on his way to the ambulance. George gave him another thumbs-up and Dwayne grinned.

"Well," said Josh. "One thing's for sure. Next year's Year 6 are going to have real trouble topping today's school trip."

DEADLINE

It was just gone six in the morning when the back door of Sam's house was kicked in.

When Sam and Karen's mum is dragged away by armed police, their whole lives change. With no clues apart from a cryptic message screamed as she leaves, the kids find themselves in a dangerous race against time to stop a bomb from exploding and save their mum's life!

£4.99
ISBN 978 14081 3110 7

Winner, Portsmouth Book Award 2012

JEAN URE

"Mr Snitcher is an alien! Pass it on..."

Nobody knew where the rumour came from. Most
of the boys think it's a joke. But the more Joe and
Harry and their friends think about it, the weirder
Mr Snitcher starts to look. Is he really an alien? And
how about the rest of the teachers?

£4.99
ISBN 978 14081 5267 6

The Gorgle

Finn doesn't want to move to the spooky old house in the first place. Soon the strange goings-on and mysterious noises are driving him crazy - and he's driving his family crazy about it. Then he sees the creature that's been hibernating in the wardrobe...

It's a Gorgle. A bit like a moth, a bit like a hornet, and a lot like a ten-foot-tall monster from your worst nightmare. It's awake. It's hungry. And Finn is the only one who can stop it!

£4.99
ISBN 978 14081 7413 5